YOGA FOR EVERYONE

CHAIR YOGA

BY LAURA VILLANO, RYT
ILLUSTRATED BY CHRISTOS SKALTSAS

BLUE OWL
BOOKS

TIPS FOR CAREGIVERS

The practice of yoga helps us learn about our breath and body, how the two are connected, and how they can help us acknowledge our feelings without letting them overwhelm us. This awareness can help us navigate different situations at school or at home. Yoga gives us tools to be the best versions of ourselves in every situation. Plus, moving our bodies feels good!

SOCIAL AND EMOTIONAL GOALS

After reading this book, kids will be able to use their yoga practice to:

1. Become more aware of their emotions and the physical sensations they produce in the body (self-awareness).

2. Use the techniques included in the text to help manage their emotions and de-stress (self-management).

TIPS FOR PRACTICE

Encourage self-awareness and self-management with these prompts:

Before reading: Ask students to check in with themselves. How do they feel, in both mind and body?
Emotional example: What kinds of thoughts are you having?
Physical example: How does your body feel today?

During reading: Encourage students to check in as they move through the book.
Emotional example: How does it feel when you close your eyes and focus on your breathing?
Physical example: How do certain poses feel in your body?

After reading: Take time to reflect after practicing the poses.
Emotional example: How do you feel after practicing yoga?
Physical example: Are there certain poses you like or don't like?

TABLE OF CONTENTS

BEFORE YOU BEGIN YOUR PRACTICE, YOU WILL NEED:

- A sturdy chair with back support
- A prop for your feet (wooden blocks or books work well)
- Comfy clothes so you can move around easily
- Water to stay hydrated
- A good attitude and an open mind!

By practicing the poses in this book, you understand any physical activity has some risk of injury.
If you experience pain or discomfort, please listen to your body, discontinue activity, and ask for help.

WHAT IS YOGA?

Yoga is a **sequence** of breathing and movements. It is good exercise for the body. It is also good exercise for the mind!

chair

Chair yoga uses a chair for balance and support. Do you want to try chair yoga?

LET'S PRACTICE!

- ❱ Find a comfortable position in your chair.

- ❱ Rest your feet flat on the floor.

- ❱ Make sure your back is straight.

props · · · · ·

TIP: If your feet don't reach the floor, you can use a **prop**.

- ❯ Put your hands on your stomach.

- ❯ **Inhale** through your nose. Feel the air fill your belly.

- ❯ **Exhale** through your nose. Feel your belly relax.

- ❯ Repeat this exercise 10 times.

TIP: Try closing your eyes during your practice. If you do not feel comfortable with your eyes closed, find an object nearby. **Focus** your eyes on that object.

Breathing is a very important part of yoga. Use your breath to move through your **poses** slowly and **intentionally**.

❯ Inhale through your nose. Reach your arms over your head.

❯ Exhale and lower your arms back to your sides.

❯ Repeat these movements 3 to 5 times.

DID YOU KNOW?

Yoga was developed more than 5,000 years ago in India. It is now a popular practice all around the world.

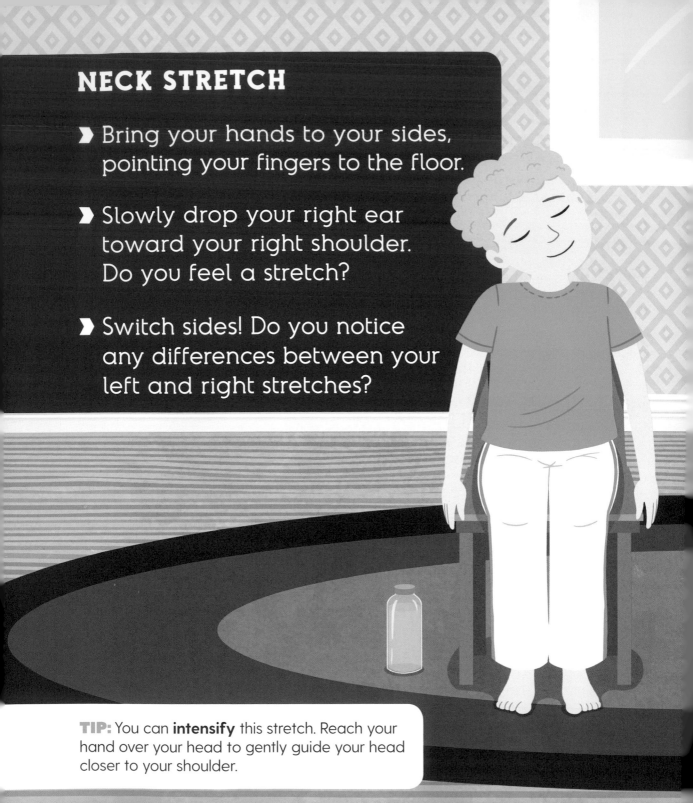

NECK STRETCH

❯ Bring your hands to your sides, pointing your fingers to the floor.

❯ Slowly drop your right ear toward your right shoulder. Do you feel a stretch?

❯ Switch sides! Do you notice any differences between your left and right stretches?

TIP: You can **intensify** this stretch. Reach your hand over your head to gently guide your head closer to your shoulder.

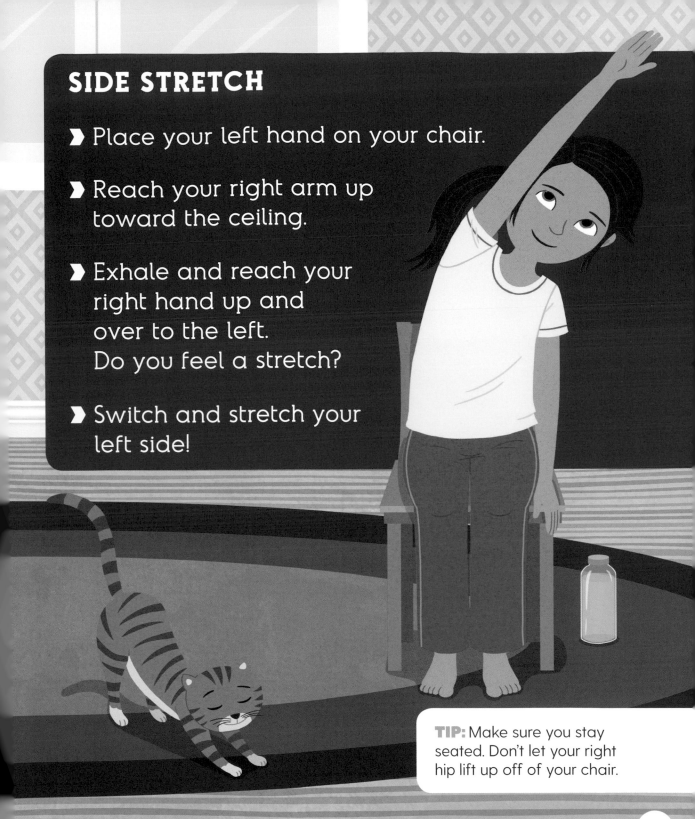

SIDE STRETCH

❯ Place your left hand on your chair.

❯ Reach your right arm up toward the ceiling.

❯ Exhale and reach your right hand up and over to the left. Do you feel a stretch?

❯ Switch and stretch your left side!

TIP: Make sure you stay seated. Don't let your right hip lift up off of your chair.

SEATED TWIST

▶ Sit tall in your chair and reach your arms up to the sky.

▶ Twist your body to the right.

▶ Bring your left hand down to your right knee. Rest your right hand on the chair behind your back.

▶ Look over your right shoulder.

▶ Breathe in and out 5 times.

▶ Switch sides and twist to your left!

DID YOU KNOW?

The most common benefits of yoga are:

· muscle building
· better sleep
· improved focus
· increased **flexibility**
· immune system boost

TIP: Move slowly and be careful. Only do what feels good for your body.

SHOULDER STRETCH PART 1

> Bring your right arm up toward the ceiling.

> Drop your right hand to the back of your neck so your elbow points up.

> Place your left hand on your right elbow. Do you feel the stretch? Now switch sides!

TIP: Keep your back straight. Don't let your ribs or belly stick out.

SHOULDER STRETCH PART 2

❯ Reach your right arm across your body.

❯ Hold your right forearm with your left hand and pull your right arm closer to your body.

❯ Now switch and stretch your left side!

SEATED PIGEON POSE

❯ Sit tall in your chair.

❯ Bring your left ankle
  to rest on top of your
  right knee. Do you feel
  a stretch in your hip?

❯ Switch sides! Notice the
  differences between your
  left and right sides.

TIP: Do you want a bigger stretch? Use your hand to gently guide your knee closer to the floor.

CAT POSE

❱ Bring your hands to your knees.

❱ Draw your shoulders back and push your chest forward.

❱ Inhale and gently look up toward the sky.

COW POSE

❯ Breathe out and round your back.

❯ Tuck your chin to your chest and look at your belly.

❯ Repeat Cat and Cow Pose 5 times.

CHAPTER 3

REFLECT

Now it is time to finish your chair yoga practice. Find a comfortable seat in your chair and close your eyes.

Take a deep breath in.
Let it out. Repeat this 5 times.

Open your eyes.
Namaste (nah-mah-stay)!
How do you feel?

GOALS AND TOOLS

GROW WITH GOALS

Practice bringing yoga into your everyday life. This can look different for everyone. Here are some ideas to get you started. You can set your own goals, too! Share your goals with your friends! Friends help us stay on track and accomplish our goals!

1. Start each day by focusing on your breath. When you take a seat at your desk in the morning, close your eyes and place your hand on your belly. Count 10 breaths.

2. When you come back to your class after lunch, practice your favorite chair yoga poses. Try this 2 times a week!

WRITING REFLECTION

Take time before and after your chair yoga practice to notice how you feel.

1. How does your body feel before yoga? What do you notice?

2. Where in your body do you feel your breath?

3. Do you notice any emotions during your yoga practice? What are they?

4. How do you feel after practicing chair yoga? Does your body feel different? Have any of your emotions changed?

GLOSSARY

exhale
To breathe out.

flexibility
The ability to bend.

focus
To concentrate on something.

inhale
To breathe in.

intensify
To make something stronger
or more powerful.

intentionally
On purpose.

namaste
A common greeting in yoga.
It means, "The spirit in me honors
and acknowledges the spirit in you."

poses
Positions or postures.

prop
Something used as support.

sequence
A series or collection of
things that follow each other
in a particular order.

yoga
A system of exercises and
meditation that helps people
control their minds and bodies
and become physically fit.

TO LEARN MORE

Finding more information is as easy as 1, 2, 3.

1. Go to www.factsurfer.com

2. Enter "**chairyoga**" into the search box.

3. Choose your cover to see a list of websites.

INDEX

Blue Owl Books are published by Jump!, 5357 Penn Avenue South, Minneapolis, MN 55419, www.jumplibrary.com

Copyright © 2020 Jump! International copyright reserved in all countries. No part of this book may be reproduced in any form without written permission from the publisher.

Library of Congress Cataloging-in-Publication Data

Names: Villano, Laura, author.
Title: Chair yoga / Laura Villano.
Description: Minneapolis, MN: Jump!, Inc., [2020]
Series: Yoga for everyone | "Blue Owl Books are published by Jump!"
Includes bibliographical references and index.
Audience: Ages 7–10.
Identifiers: LCCN 2019028034 (print)
LCCN 2019028035 (ebook)
ISBN 9781645271840 (hardcover)
ISBN 9781645271857 (paperback)
ISBN 9781645271864 (ebook)
Subjects: LCSH: Hatha yoga—Juvenile literature. | Hatha yoga for children.
Classification: LCC RA781.7 .V557 2020 (print)
LCC RA781.7 (ebook)
DDC 613.7/046—dc23
LC record available at https://lccn.loc.gov/2019028034
LC ebook record available at https://lccn.loc.gov/2019028035

Editor: Jenna Trnka
Designer: Anna Peterson
Illustrator: Christos Skaltsas

Printed in the United States of America at Corporate Graphics in North Mankato, Minnesota.